13 Legends of Fire Island
and the Great South Bay

Jack Whitehouse

iUniverse, Inc.
New York   Bloomington

13 Legends of Fire Island

and the Great South Bay

iUniverse books may be ordered through booksellers or by contacting:

iUniverse
1663 Liberty Drive
Bloomington, IN 47403
www.iuniverse.com
1-800-Authors (1-800-288-4677)

Because of the dynamic nature of the Internet, any Web addresses or links
contained in this book may have changed since publication and may no
longer be valid. The views expressed in this work are solely those of the
author and do not necessarily reflect the views of the publisher, and the
publisher hereby disclaims any responsibility for them.

ISBN: 978-1-4401-0203-5 (pbk)
ISBN: 978-1-4401-0202-8 (ebk)

Printed in the United States of America

iUniverse Rev. 11/25/08

To all the people who made these legends come to life.

Acknowledgements

Many people helped me during the course of my research and while writing *13 Legends of Fire Island and the Great South Bay*. First, I would like to thank the founder of the *Fire Island Tide*, Mr. Warren C. McDowell. Warren not only provided the venue for the initial publication of this short story collection but also the advice, guidance and often the background information necessary to complete many of the stories.

Instrumental in making this book a reality is the current publisher of the *Fire Island Tide Newspaper, Inc.,* Kate Heissenbuttel and her husband Hank. Likewise, I am indebted to the *Tide's* Art Director Linda Grant for her expertise in providing the illustrations that accompanied the original publication of these stories.

A few of the stories are thanks to the past research and writings of some great local historians and authors. Madeleine C. Johnson's book *Fire Island 1650s-1980s* was both an inspiration and a source of invaluable information. Likewise, Harry Havemeyer's *Fire Island's Surf Hotel and other Hostelries on Fire Island Beaches in the Nineteenth Century* and *East On the Great South Bay Sayville and Bellport 1860-1960* provided information about Fire Island's past. Historian Douglas Tuomey who in the 1950s and 1960s contributed many fine stories to the *Long Island Forum* is another invaluable reference, and finally, the writings of Edward Richard Shaw, particularly his book *Legends of Fire Island Beach and The South Side,* was an important resource.

I must thank members of the Sayville Historical Society for their input and assistance. The Society's President, Constance Curry, Curator Linda Conron and Program Chair Suzanne Robilotta were of great help with this and other research projects. I also want to thank the irrepressibly upbeat Society member John Wells for his encouragement in getting this and other projects completed.

The Long Island Maritime Museum staff, particularly Barbara Forde, Betty Ann Arink and Arlene Balcewicz, deserves thanks for their quick and able assistance in helping me track down many nautical details of Sayville's maritime history.

Rob and Jean DeVito of St. George's Manor went above and beyond what was required in providing their own personal narrative of the history of the property as well as affording me the opportunity to thoroughly review their facility.

A special thank you to my good friend, Islip Town Councilman Christopher Bodkin, for his knowledge of the town, his erudite conversation, and for providing local texts that would otherwise not have been available to me.

Thanks also go to Acting Superintendent Sean McGuinness and the entire staff of the Fire Island National Seashore for their combined and continuing efforts to preserve Fire Island and much of the South Shore Estuary for future generations.

Special thanks must also go to next-door neighbor and life long Sayville residents Al Bergen and his wife Lois. Their descriptions of life in Sayville in the 1930s, local sailing clubs and the like were invaluable, as was their encouragement as I pursued this project.

No book about Fire Island and the Great South Bay would be complete without recognition of the contribution made by the ferry services. The Stein family, particularly Judy and Ken III and their fifth-generation Sayville Ferry Service never fail to provide a helping hand.

I must thank lifelong resident of Sayville, lifelong friend and recent running buddy Bill Griek for his moral support, his leads to interesting local bay people and his always upbeat and positive influence.

Thank you to librarian Jeanne Demmers who located and provided me with many hard to find books on Long Island history.

I want to thank the staff of the Sayville library, particularly Jonathan Pryer and Allan Heid, for their always friendly and able assistance. Also, Mark Rothenberg at the Celia M. Hastings Local History Room at the Patchogue library for his extra efforts in helping me to conduct my research.

David Griese, Director of the Fire Island Lighthouse, helped greatly with details of the history of the lighthouse and answers to many questions about the people and events that shaped that part of Fire Island.

My mother, Elizabeth Catlin Whitehouse, who spent much of her life in and around the Great South Bay and Fire Island, deserves recognition for providing her input on events as she remembered them.

I want to thank my son John III and his wife Etsu for their support, particularly with the technical aspects involved in the publication, research and presentation of the material.

Most of all I want to thank the award-winning editor of the *Fire Island Tide Newspaper, Inc.,* my wife of more than forty years, Elaine, for her editorial assistance and for her steadfast belief in my seeing the project through to completion. The book would not have been possible without her.

Contents

Two Brutal Women and the Famous Money Ship of Fire Island

The "two brutal women" of Fire Island were not the first, nor the most notorious, female pirates to terrorize parts of the U.S. eastern seaboard and the Caribbean, but they were surely some of the most effective at their chosen profession. Anne Bonny, the beautiful girlfriend of pirate "Calico Jack" Rackham aboard the *Revenge*, did her dirty work as early as the 1700s. Fire Island's two women pirates plundered and killed almost a century later, well into the middle of the 19th century before leaving the beach to live out west in comfortable retirement.

So who were these female pirates? While the two were reportedly quite intelligent and in excellent physical and mental condition, Lydia Jones and Portentia Riley earned their moniker "two brutal women" by virtue of their ruthlessness. They had to be ruthless in order to steal cargo, kill men much bigger than themselves, and sell their ill-gotten gains for profit.

If there was something odd about them, it was that two such competent and attractive women chose to live year round without benefit of friend or neighbor. In fact, the closest neighbor to their oceanfront redoubt was also their sometime competitor, another infamous sand pirate of the time, Mr. Jeremiah Smith. From just after the end of the Revolutionary War, the evil Mr. Smith conducted decades of wrongdoings from his self-constructed home at Cherry Grove, luring passing ships into wrecking on the shore, stabbing to death any survivors, and taking whatever he was able to steal to the markets of New York City. But as bad as he was, Mr. Jeremiah Smith knew to keep his distance from the two brutal women who lived only about three miles east of him, close to where the center of Fire Island Pines is located today.

Were it not for the grounding of one particular ship, known only as the "Money Ship" for its precious pirate cargo of gold and silver, history might not recognize Lydia and Portentia for their brutality, treachery and greed, but there was such a vessel and thus have they become known. This is the story of the female pirates and why gold coins are found even to this day on the ocean beaches of Fire Island.

The women had one purported friend, but he was as much a phantom as a moon shadow on a cloudy night. Known to history only as "the dark-visaged man," he served as the women's fence, periodically visiting the beach to collect the cargo he would bring to the city and sell for a huge profit.

Records show that in the early summer of 1816, the dark-faced man put ashore at Montauk Point, having arrived there on a treasure-laden pirate ship captained by a man later identified as Mr. John Sloane. The pirate ship mirrored Sloane's movements along the coast as he made his way by land to the women's home on Fire Island. When he received his signal from the dark-faced man, Captain Sloane lowered two longboats into the sea taking his entire pirate crew with him to the beach. The idea was to deliver their treasure for safekeeping to Lydia Jones and Portentia Riley until such time as the dark-faced man could move the booty safely to the mainland.

The story is murky on precisely what happened next, but the most accepted version is that an extremely high surf engulfed both longboats, causing them to breach and tossing everyone into the stormy sea. Whether all fifteen men died from drowning because their pockets were full of treasure, or were murdered by the women and their dark-faced friend for the very same treasure, is unclear. But what is a matter of record is that Captain Sloane and his cabin boy, the young Thomas Knight, somehow survived. In the confusion, Sloane and Knight made their way down the beach where they hid for days in the swale between the dunes, avoiding the local constabulary that had come to investigate the presence of this mysterious sailing ship anchored off the great barrier beach. Long suspected of foul play, the authorities quickly arrested Lydia and Portentia and took them off to the mainland for questioning.

Following the departure of the authorities, pirate Captain Sloane and young Tom Knight reestablished contact with the dark-faced man. The three agreed to divide equally the gold and silver treasure collected from the pockets of the dead pirate crew. Using three large and identical blue china crocks, they buried their individual fortunes -- most of it in Spanish gold coin -- in separate locations on the dunes.

In the meantime, in the rough wind and sea conditions, the unmanned pirate ship had begun to drag anchor and was moving slowly down the coast in an easterly direction. When she had gotten as far as Southampton, local folks took notice and boarded the ship to investigate. They discovered she was abandoned, carried no name, held no cargo and was without a ship's log or record of any kind. All they found was a variety of weapons and one Spanish silver dollar.

Eventually the ship was put up for auction and sold to a salvage company for the wood. But before that happened, the mysterious pirate ship provided one more surprise. Two curious seamen from Southampton, a whaleman named Henry Green and another named Franklin Jagger one evening went aboard the abandoned ship to look around. While in the captain's cabin Mr. Green's eye caught the reflection of a bright object in the overhead. Pulling away a loose ceiling tile, silver coins came tumbling out like sand through the navigator's hourglass. In their excitement, the men filled their pockets to overflowing, but lost the light from their oil lamp and so were unable to keep track of a good portion of their find, losing much of it into the sea.

What happened to the two brutal women, Lydia and Portentia? The authorities released them after only one or two days for lack of evidence. Long practiced at deceiving the authorities, the two managed to keep their murderous deeds and ill-gotten gold and silver from official notice. They were still young, with much of life left to enjoy, so they took their wealth, pulled up stakes, and moved out west.

And so it was that silver and gold coins found their way to the beach, and are still discovered even up to the present day. According to Madeleine C. Johnson in her book, *Fire Island 1650s-1980s*, the most recent known find was by one Zea Hopkins in 1955.

How much treasure from the "Money Ship" is still out there remains a mystery. We know the blue crock containing the gold buried by the cabin boy Thomas Knight was found by a knowledgeable and dedicated treasure seeker some forty years after it was buried. But two of the three blue crocks – each full of ancient gold coins – apparently remain buried somewhere in the beautiful beaches near Fire Island Pines.

The Watch Hill Stone

I looked it up –the date was Saturday, the 4th of September 1954. That was the day my father took my mother and us children to Fire Island to survey the damage caused by Hurricane Carol, one of the worst hurricanes ever to hit Long Island. The storm had struck on the Tuesday before, with winds of well over 100 mph, tearing up the fragile barrier beach, and in some places removing layers of sand put down by Nature centuries before. As experienced beachcombers know, it is after such devastating storms that secrets from the past can suddenly see the light of day, if ever so briefly, before disappearing once more.

By Saturday noon we had anchored our 28-foot Richardson in about two feet of water just west of Watch Hill, the approximate geographical middle of Fire Island. After a bay side picnic – my mother had long ago learned that armies weren't the only organizations that traveled on their stomachs -- we began our trek to the ocean.

Damage to the bay shoreline had been minimal, with hardly a sign of the massively destructive force of four days before. Wading ashore, the bay bottom was clearly visible, thick with large crabs sliding about in the shiny eelgrass, stalking the weakest within schools of fat and slow moving killies. My father explained that despite the numerous and destructive nor'easters and occasional hurricanes like Carol, the Great South Bay had remained essentially unchanged for the past 2000 years. Scientists believed it was about 200 B.C. when a major, high-energy event created the bay -- actually a lagoon -- from the swampy morass it had been for hundreds or even thousands, of years before that.

But we were shocked when we saw the ocean beach. Instead of a graded beach, the shoreline was flat. At high tide the smallest waves could run right up to the base of what remained of the dunes, which looked as if some giant knife blade had cut them vertically in half. On the flat expanse of sand there was not much to find except a few boards, timbers, wires and other flotsam and jetsam from crushed wooden boats, boardwalks and beach houses.

Towards late afternoon, as we were coming back east toward Watch Hill, my father noticed the edge of an odd outcropping, about ten to twelve feet up, on the sheer sand facade of the highest dune. Closer examination revealed it to be the leading edge of a flat rock, about one inch thick, about eight square feet in size. The stone had some strange writing scratched into it, both on the face and on the narrow sides. The writing included letters and figures, each about one inch high. My father said he had not seen such writing before. He tried to pull it down for closer examination, but it was stuck fast and too high up for us to gain sufficient leverage to unseat it. So we left the stone where we found it, vowing to return another day, equipped for a better look. But as those things go, we did not return that season, and eventually thought little more about our odd discovery.

Many years passed before I began to think more seriously about what we had found. After all, such stone inscription could not have been the work of a child, and the stone's location seemed to rule out it being a hoax. So what was it? Finally, when I retired, I found both the time and opportunity to do some research. Systematically going through a vast amount of historical and archaeological data, I pieced together what I believe is the story behind what we called the Watch Hill Stone.

I learned that the Icelandic sagas say that in 986 A.D. a Norse explorer and merchant named Herjolfson ran into a fierce Atlantic storm while trying to get from Iceland to Eric the Red's Greenland settlement. The storm drove Herjolfson's longboat far to the west, close to a heavily wooded shore that scholars today believe was probably the northern tip of Newfoundland.

The lost explorer found his way back to Greenland and described his accidental journey to all who would listen. Leif Ericsson, the teenage son of the infamous Eric the Red, took note, and years later, in about 1001, gathered an expedition to retrace Herjolfsson's route.

The sagas say that on his initial voyage, Ericsson and his longboat crew of about fifty men discovered three separate areas on the North American continent. He named them as follows: *Helluland*, meaning "land of the flat stones"; *Markland*, or "forest land"; and *Vinland*, meaning "Wine Land." The precise location of the three areas has always been unclear; however, many historians identify *Helluland* as Baffin Island and *Markland* as Labrador. But *Vinland* remains a bigger question.

Historians know Ericson named *Vinland* for its bountiful wild fruit, particularly wild grapes and other such species easily converted into alcoholic drink. So *Vinland* almost certainly lay south of the Gulf of St. Lawrence, the approximate northern limit for such plants. Many scholars believe that Nova Scotia, the states bordering the Gulf of Maine, and those regions as far south as the bays of New York might well have been part of *Vinland*.

In 1960, archaeologists unearthed the Norse settlement at *L'Anse aux Meadows* on the northern tip of Newfoundland, proving that Leif Ericson and other Norse that followed him had been at least that far south. The camp once housed 135 men, 15 women and a variety of livestock. The Norse inhabited the site for several years, perhaps much longer. Problems associated with having so few women present seem to have led to the camp's eventual abandonment. Anthropologists also now argue that the Norse probably had more settlements, even further south and west, that have yet to be found. A growing body of evidence shows that these ancient explorers probably traveled as far west as Minnesota -- through the St. Lawrence Seaway and the Great Lakes -- and as far down the east coast as the Hudson River.

A look the Atlantic Ocean currents shows how easy it would have been for a Norse longboat to travel from *L'Anse aux Meadows* to the mouth of the Hudson River. The Labrador Current runs down the west side of Newfoundland to the mouth of the St. Lawrence River, and then basically carries south all the way to Montauk Point, along the coast of Fire Island to New York Bay. Leif Ericsson's longboat, traveling with a favorable wind, might have easily logged 15 knots per hour, so the voyage to New York harbor would not have taken all that long.

But travel by longboat was for the sturdy, not the weak. The Norse built these shallow draft, highly seaworthy craft with a sealed main deck and no cover from the elements. Thus, the Norsemen tried to sail only during the warmer weather, in daylight hours, and within sight of land. Depending on conditions, these master mariners either anchored in still water for the night or pulled their longboat ashore for greater cover. Sometimes they used the longboat's linen sail to make a tent to sleep under, or if it was safer, they might go ashore and pitch wool tents brought with them for the journey. If the voyage required them to be at sea overnight, they slept on deck under blankets or two-man sleeping bags made of animal skin.

The ancient Norse mariners used hand-held drop-lines to catch codfish. Dried, smoked or fresh cod provided much of their at-sea diet. Certainly the ready availability of cod and other species off the northeast coast of the U.S. would have eased the hardship of Leif Ericson's and his successors exploratory travels.

What is the other evidence of ancient Norse travels in the area? A Norse penny found at a significant Native American archaeological site in Penobscot Bay, Maine in 1957, has been authenticated as a Norwegian coin minted sometime between 1065 and 1080 A.D. The cartographic records from two of the earliest explorers of the New England area, Verrazano in 1524 and Mercator in 1569, show the existence of a large stone tower at Newport, Rhode Island. Then there are the rune stones.

Rune stones are flat slabs of stone on which ancient Scandinavian letters, or runes, were carved. The most famous of these is the Kensington rune stone found by a Minnesota farmer in 1898. This remarkable stone shows that the Norse reached the middle of North America in the 11th century. Initially dismissed as a hoax, the Kensington stone has become accepted by scholars as genuine after recent study of additional examples of ancient rune texts.

A recent direct translation of the inscription on the Kensington stone reads:

Eight Goths (Swedes) *and 22 Norwegians on discovery voyage from Vinland over west we had camp by two skerries one day's journey north from this stone we were and fished one day after we came home found ten men red with blood and dead A(ve) V(irgo) M(aria) preserve from evil.*

More than 100 rune stones have been found on the New England coast including that of the Long Island Sound. Of all the stones found, only one has ever been shown to be a hoax.

What grieves me is that my father could have added greatly to that body of evidence proving that the ancient Norse traveled as far south as New York harbor – or at least the middle of Fire Island. If only he had managed to pry the Watch Hill stone loose! It all makes sense. The ancient Norse probably used the Watch Hill area as the equivalent of a rest stop. It was a place where they could spend the night without much fear of attack from the Indians, gain a good view of the surrounding land and sea, hunt game, collect wild berries and catch fish. But unless the Watch Hill stone is unearthed again, we probably will never know for sure.

The Terrorist

 You are my old and dearest friend, but there is something even you don't know about me that I must get off my chest before I die. I never told you before now because I was afraid, but there is nothing I need fear from anyone any longer. After I'm gone, feel free to repeat any, or all, of my story. But I believe my secret will die with you, still a secret.

Contrary to what you think, I am not an American. My name isn't even the name by which you know me. I was born in Leipzig not long after World War I; my mother was a U.S. Army nurse and my father a minor German official in the post-war German government. We spoke American English at home, and so I grew up with native fluency in both German and American. In 1939, at the age of 18, like every other good German youth, I wanted to join the *Wehrmacht*, and so I did. I performed my military duties with distinction. I was more German than the Fuhrer. I was so outstanding that before long I came to the attention of the powerful Central Security Service (CSS), a part of which would later become the infamous Gestapo.

The CSS liked me because I was smart, strong, a patriotic and dedicated German who knew how to take orders and, perhaps most importantly, I could speak fluent American English. I was so proud that they chose me for one of their most secret training programs. My unit was run by the foreign intelligence branch of the *Abwehr*, directly under the control of German High Command. I spent almost two years learning special communications procedures, how to operate behind enemy lines, bomb-making and sabotage techniques and other such skills needed for participating in the secret war in America.

In April 1942, a group of six highly trained men, myself included, went aboard U-584 for the long and painfully slow passage from Germany to the east coast of the U.S. It was a miserable trip. We were cramped with six extra men aboard and the time passed very slowly with nothing for us to do. Inside the submarine was freezing because of the frigid North Atlantic waters. All of us bundled up in snowsuits to stay warm. But we eventually made it to the U.S. east coast and without once being detected by any allied forces.

A little before midnight on Saturday, June 13th 1942, we were finally ready to make our way ashore and step into our clandestine roles in the secret German war on the U.S.

In a dense fog and a mirror-flat sea, the Captain brought his submarine to within a couple of hundred meters of the Amagansett beach. It was here, in a small rubber raft deployed from the sub, that our German team began their mission to sabotage East Coast war industries. Grumman Aircraft in Bethpage, the major Long Island Rail Road terminals, and Floyd Bennett Field were among the vital U.S. infrastructure targets on our list.

Now you are probably thinking to yourself that the old fool has gotten it wrong. Everyone has heard the famous story of the German saboteurs landing on the beach at Amagansett and almost everyone knows the saboteurs were four in number, not six.

That much is true. But what no one knows, until you are hearing it now, is that U-584, made another stop that night. In the wee hours of Sunday morning, June 14th, with the fog still unrelenting, two more agents went ashore on Fire Island, not at Amagansett, but at Sunken Forest, near Cherry Grove. I was one of those agents.

The plan was for the Amagansett team to work inland immediately after hitting the beach, trying to meld into the German community in the area. Our plan was different. We were the best American speakers and they wanted to use that to advantage. We were to hide out in the unique, dense forest foliage just behind the main dunes at Sunken Forest until the first opportunity came along to blend into the summer beach crowd at Cherry Grove.

You remember the Sunken Forest back then, much like a woods from out of a Grimm's fairy tale. It served as perfect protection for men on a mission such as ours. One could only enter the place through the dunes on the ocean side because the swampy morass on the north side made entry from the bay very unpleasant, if not impossible. So our backs were covered.

Our plan worked well. Immediately after getting ashore we dug ourselves into a low-lying spot behind one of the dunes near a particularly thick stand of holly. Using wood from cases we had brought ashore and driftwood found on the beach, we worked well into the morning hours making a substantial, well-concealed shelter. Inside we stashed our plans, commo gear, weapons, and a considerable amount of U.S. currency, thinking we could return to retrieve it when we needed to.

Dressed in American-made bathing suits we had brought along, and carrying small beach bags with another change of clothes, we were able to leave the area late that same afternoon. As planned, we blended in with a bunch of day-trippers on an early evening ferry back to Sayville.

No one seemed to take notice of us as anything but summer tourists. Of course, in a situation such as this, your mind can play tricks on you. You are living a complete lie and so you feel sort of like you're naked and that others can see who you really are. At one point the ferryboat proprietor, a keen observer of his clientele, seemed suspicious of us. But he did not take steps, at least of any notice to us, to intervene. I mention this because it was the only time anyone ever seemed to doubt my American identity.

From the ferry terminal we walked the mile or so to the Lafayette Hotel on Candee Avenue where, masquerading as summer visitors from New York City, we booked rooms.

Less than two weeks later, FBI Director J. Edgar Hoover, made headlines nationwide when he announced that all eight German agents who had landed on U.S. beaches had been arrested. You may or may not recall that on June 17th, U-202 landed four German agents at Ponte Vedra Beach, just south of Jacksonville, Florida. Our team was unaware of this other group until Hoover's announcement.

For my colleague and myself, Hoover's public chest beating meant a great deal. Hoover's words put us in lock down. As previously instructed, we were forbidden to conduct any sabotage action until told to resume operations by the High Command.

Weeks passed, and as had been pre-arranged, my colleague and I split up. I don't know whatever happened to him, I never saw or heard of him again. I moved into New York City and got a defense industry-related job using one of the aliases set up for me. The alias is the name by which you have known me these many years.

The High Command did not re-contact me, and I have no idea why not. Perhaps they thought I had been doubled by the FBI, or maybe they had negative reporting about me from someone else. Who knows? The possibilities are endless. That's why it's called the looking-glass wars.

At first I returned to Cherry Grove and Sunken Forest on a couple of occasions, but no message ever came. As far as I know, to this day our hideout remains in place. Money, maps, plans, all of it is still there; at least I've never read of anyone discovering it.

So, the war came to an end. As time passed, I grew more and more apprehensive at the possibility that a knock on the door might still come. In the 1950's and '60's, even into the late '80's, I was consumed by the fear that the East German *Stasi,* the dreaded East German State Security Service, would try to use me. But they never did. Evidently that horrible spymaster, Marcus Wolf, simply wasn't interested.

In 1989 the Berlin wall fell, and at last I began to feel safe. Then I read that the *Stasi* hadn't destroyed all their files and my personal feeling of terror returned. What if my file was discovered? Would not the FBI come for me, even after all this time? Would I be spending my final years in prison? How ironic, I kept thinking. I came here to terrorize, and ended up being terrorized, not by my innocent targets but by myself. But no one ever came, and now I am dying.

So, my old friend, what do you think? Do you believe me? And if you believe me, do you judge me harshly? Will you write about me in your newspaper?

No, as I said at the start, I think not. I think you've already decided my story isn't worth the troubles you would bring upon yourself in repeating it. You also understand that your treasured Sunken Forest would be destroyed by those seeking another kind of treasure -- people digging everywhere trying to find all that gear and money we left behind so many years ago. No, I think my secret is safe with you.

The Grasping Hands

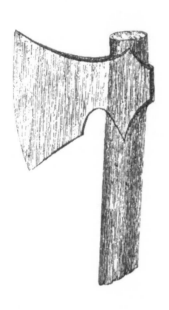

That there was piracy on Fire Island, both shore and sea based, is a well-known fact. The discovery in many places of buried gold and silver coins and other treasure of all sorts, as well as the chronicling of credible eye witness accounts has left no doubt that Fire Island and the surrounding waters all suffered from the scourge of those who sailed under the black flag's skull and bones.

The pirate stories that have come down to us read, for the most part, like romantic fantasy, describing great treasure and wild characters but providing few examples of how vicious pirates could be. But as local historian Douglas Tuomey discovered, one story from 225 years ago is an exception to that general rule, a horror story even by today's standards. The local pirate "Handy Jones" -- his true identity apparently known only to himself and one other -- just might have been the New World's first serial killer.

In 1780, the waterways were the highways of today, moving all manner of travelers -- fur-trappers, fishermen, and merchants -- and their goods. This floating wealth naturally attracted water borne thieves; pirate attacks were quite commonplace. Escape for the scoundrels from the scene of the crime -- loot in hand -- was easy. River ruffians had a choice of escaping to either bank, down river or upstream. Sand pirates had no witnesses to their work done on the barren empty beaches. Ocean-going lawbreakers simply disappeared over the horizon. Pirates, especially the small-time perpetrators, had little to fear from law enforcement because in those days the resources to identify, track down and prosecute them were almost non-existent.

In 1780-81, historians estimate that only about two to three hundred men made their living on the 64,000 acres of water between Fire Island and the mainland. These men worked alone, on small, shallow draft sloops, using nets, tongs, rakes and other such equipment to harvest their catch. Occasionally a man would be lost to illness, injury or accident, but almost always both his body and his boat would eventually be found. But then in 1780, the first of the disappearances began.

In a ten-month period, three fishing boats vanished. One fisherman was never found; one was found near today's Fire Island Pines and the third just off Bay Shore. Those who discovered the first body, near Fire Island, concluded that the man had died from loss of blood due to some freak accident. Something had happened to cause him to lose both hands cleanly at the wrists. They surmised that his boat must have sunk or possibly drifted out the inlet never to be seen again.

Suspicion that foul play might somehow be involved in the disappearance of all three fishermen came months later with the finding of the second body in Great Cove off Bay Shore. It, too, had only cleanly cut stumps where the hands had once been, but there was more. This man's face was frozen in a look of horror. His boat was also nowhere to be found.

As the months passed, more boats mysteriously disappeared with their owners eventually washing up on the beach, or found in the bay, all missing at least one hand, or arm, and usually both.

The South Shore baymen developed a theory about what was happening. They decided that somehow, some unknown person went to sea with each of the victims. Despite the fact that the fishermen worked alone, and despite awareness of the problem on the part of everyone, somehow this mysterious killer was able to put to sea without arousing the suspicion of any of his victims. Somehow he was also able to overpower these strong men and cut off their hands almost as though they held them out for the cleaving. How could this be and where were the missing boats?

Gallows humor allowed the baymen and their families to provide this mysterious attacker with a grim moniker. They called him the pirate "Handy Jones." They figured that whoever Handy Jones really was, he almost certainly must be a non-suspicious and trusted fellow, perhaps even one of their own. He might be a neighbor, a town merchant or any man local people knew and trusted. How else could he get aboard the boats, surprise his target and then successfully torture and kill him in such hideous manner?

Or else, they figured, Handy Jones might just be an extremely cunning person. He might follow a suitable victim for some time to determine the pattern of his habits and behavior. His homework done, he would then board his intended victim's boat and under cover of darkness hide himself in the hold. Most bay sloops were of similar design with a large hold for the catch and two access hatches making it relatively easy to hide. The men thought Handy

Jones might then remain concealed until he was sure the boat was well off shore, or until he heard the anchor let go. At just the right moment he would emerge from his hiding place and rush the shocked bayman, pitching him into the water.

In the described scenario, preoccupation, surprise, and panic would all work in favor of Handy Jones. Each startled boat owner would react in the same way. Shocked, confused and suddenly submerged in the water, each would come to the water's surface and make for the nearest gunwale of his boat in order to pull himself up. It was then that Handy Jones would strike, raising his broadax, sword or machete and gleefully bring it down on one or both of the grasping hands. No one could last very long after that. They would quickly bleed to death or drown. Most men shuddered at the thought that Handy Jones probably enjoyed watching every last second of his poor victims' tortured deaths.

As for the missing boats, the men surmised that as with any pirate, Handy Jones sailed off with his prize, probably out one of the inlets to the New England shore or to New Jersey or up the Hudson. In 1780-81, without the requirement of a license or even ownership papers of any kind, Handy Jones could safely sell the stolen craft for good money with no questions asked.

The story is unclear about precisely how the gruesome murders finally ended, but end they did, and abruptly so. The story involves the older brother of one of the pirate's early victims. The brave, vengeance-driven brother decided he would appear the perfect target for the murderous pirate and lure Handy Jones into a trap. To this end he docked his boat in a remote location and each day fished out of sight of any other craft. Finally, one morning he noticed telltale shoeprints in the mud near where his boat lay moored.

He set sail and calmly and deliberately made for a lonely spot in the middle of the bay where he prepared to drop anchor. Knowing that his brother's murderer almost certainly lay hidden just under his feet, ready to attack, he kept all his senses on extreme alert. He strained continuously to sense any motion or sound out of the ordinary, anything that would signal the emergence from hiding of the stealthy Handy Jones.

The fatal rush came not long after the anchor caught and held. Handy Jones seemingly came out of nowhere flying toward him at full speed. But this time the pirate's intended victim was ready, and side stepped the rush sending Handy Jones headlong into the bay.

Handy Jones, shocked, surprised and panicked as his victims had been, did what they had done. He reflexively made for the low side of the boat. As he rose from the water grasping the gunwale, the vengeance-seeker swung his own sharpened ax. As the blade came arching down, his eyes focused horrified on a face he knew very well, but too late to stop the blow.

When the handless body of the beloved town doctor was found, the village was aghast. But the killings finally stopped, and years later, when no other victims were found, it was assumed that Handy Jones had died. Only one man knew that Handy Jones was, in fact, the last victim.

The Spirit of Margaret Fuller

Please, come in and sit down. Our police send people like you to talk to me and I am happy that they do. You see, I can explain what you experienced where it is simply not possible for them to do so. Oh, mind you, the police don't send many people to me. In fact, it seems I can hardly remember my last caller, but then maybe that's more a result of old age than actual time passed.

Let me begin by telling you that the police gave me only your name and profession. You are a teacher and a writer, but I confess, I know a good deal more about you than that. You are intelligent and a romantic, you are also inquisitive, optimistic and enthusiastic. You believe in individualism and the primacy of the human spirit, and you find comfort in the existence of a beneficent God. You want genuine equality of opportunity for all people and you have the proven interest and ability to help the world move in the direction of that goal.

Oh, please don't get me wrong, I don't mean to behave like some roadside fortuneteller predicting your future in return for monetary gain. Neither am I trying to impress you as a trained detective with powers of deduction like Sherlock Holmes. Not at all. But I can tell you from years of experience that I know Margaret Fuller, and I know the kind of people she seeks out, and what they're like.

You're probably beginning to think I'm something of a rambling old fool. Who in the world is Margaret Fuller, you are wondering, and what does all this have to do with what you saw and heard?

Please help yourself to another cup of tea, or something stronger if you like, and I will tell you, as cogently as I am able.

Almost exactly 156 years ago, on July 19, 1850, an early season storm slammed into Fire Island. A sailing ship, the Elizabeth, got caught up in it and went aground about a quarter mile off the beach directly out from where we're sitting now, near Point O' Woods.

The Elizabeth was a beautiful, newly built, three-masted barque that set sail from Italy on the 17th of May 1850 bound for New York harbor. She had on board five passengers and a crew of 14, and carried a cargo of marble, silks, liquors and other luxuries. Her passengers included Italian Count Giovanni Ossoli, his famous wife Margaret Fuller, their two-year-old son Angelino and the boy's nursemaid, a young girl named Celeste Paolini. The fifth passenger was a man named Horace Sumner.

The voyage was a disaster from the start. After only one week at sea, the ship's captain, a man named Seth Hasty, died a miserable death from the highly contagious smallpox. Upon the captain's death, the inexperienced first mate, Mr. Bangs, assumed command. Then, about two days out from Gibraltar, Margaret's two-year-old son came down with the same illness that had killed the captain. But with Margaret's constant care, Angelino survived, and was well on the road to recovery by the time the ship was approaching the port of New York. It seemed all would turn out well for Margaret but, as she had predicted in letters to friends before the journey began, it simply was not to be.

On the night of July 18th, as the ship was making its way toward New York and an anticipated docking the next day, the wind began to pick up. By midnight it had reached gale force and by 2:30 a.m. on the 19th, the inexperienced Mr. Bangs had lost his way. Less than one hour later the Elizabeth went aground. Soon afterwards, a large wave literally picked the ship up and slammed her down. This time she hit broadside against the sandbar. The force of the strike broke her in two, with only the forward portion of the ship remaining intact and above water.

None of the passengers or crew were lost or even injured in the grounding. So after some initial confusion, everyone aboard managed to come together on the forecastle.

In the early morning light, through the gloom of the storm, they could just make out people starting to gather on the shore. But no one there appeared to be mounting any sort of rescue of any kind. With their situation becoming more and more precarious, two of the ship's crew agreed to try to swim for shore to encourage a rescue attempt. Both men made it, but then the passenger, Mr. Horace Sumner, decided to try. He drowned shortly after entering the water, in plain view of the others.

As the morning wore on, people on the shore tried to launch a rescue boat. They also tried to get a line out to the ship with a line-throwing mortar. But all such attempts failed. The mountainously high seas and howling winds precluded any further shore-based rescue attempt.

Meanwhile, on the forecastle, Mr. Bangs convinced most of the remainder of the crew that their only hope lay in grabbing hold of a wooden plank and swimming for shore. But four of the crew and none of the surviving passengers would listen. Margaret and her husband knew their precious child would never make it.

Then, about 3 o'clock in the afternoon, yet another very large wave came along and destroyed what remained of the ship, flinging one and all into the sea. One or two of the crew managed to make it ashore, but no one else did. The bodies of the ship's steward and little Angelino eventually washed up on the beach, but two bodies, those of Margaret Fuller and her husband, were never found. Eventually, a large reward was offered to anyone finding the remains, but the money went unclaimed.

I can see that while you appreciate my story, you are still wondering what it all has to do with you. So, let me tell you something more about Margaret Fuller, and perhaps you will begin to understand.

At her death in 1850, Margaret Fuller was barely 40 years old and had already been described by the American intellectual community of the day as "the most important woman of the nineteenth century."

In 1816, at the age of only six, she could translate from Latin the works of Virgil and Ovid. By 12 she could quote from Shakespeare and Plato and intelligently debate points from John Locke's metaphysics. At 25 she began her exchange of ideas with the great leader of the Renaissance in American thought, the philosopher Ralph Waldo Emerson, who would serve as her supporter, mentor and guide for the rest of her life.

I will not bore you with reprising all that she wrote, or discuss the importance and daring of her works such as her 1845 book, *Woman in the Nineteenth Century*. Experts describe the book as the primer for today's American feminism in all its economic, intellectual, political and sexual aspects.

Like you, Fuller taught school and was a writer. She was editor of Emerson's transcendental movement's quarterly, and worked as the literary critic for Horace Greeley's *New York Tribune*, recognized as the most influential newspaper of its time. Her close friends included some of the greatest men of American literature, including Henry David Thoreau and Oliver Wendell Holmes. In Italy, just before her death, she served as a frontline nurse in the Italian campaign for independence.

In 1852, Ralph Waldo Emerson wrote in her memoir, "One thing only she demanded of all her friends -- they should not be satisfied with the common routine of life. They should aspire to something higher, better, holier, than they had now attained." Emerson also said, "In order to be Margaret's friend, one must be capable of seeking something – capable of some aspiration for the better."

So, perhaps by now you are beginning to understand that what you experienced that foggy morning on the beach was an apparition, indeed the living spirit of Margaret Fuller. The way you describe her quaint clothing, her intelligent eyes – yes, that was she.

At some point in your education you must have learned something about transcendentalism. You are probably familiar with Margaret's works, possibly without even realizing it. She wrote that she believed she was capable of attaining knowledge of existence that goes beyond the reach of the normal human senses. She believed that intuition and the individual conscience "transcend" experience, and are a better indication of the truth than are the senses and logical reason. So, you see, her appearance to you on the beach is not out of character, either for her, or apparently for you.

Over the years, people with whom I have spoken who have witnessed her say they do not feel as though they've seen a specter but rather a spirit. They have all described, as you have, a feeling of being uplifted, and a powerful desire to engage more fully in the experiences of their lives, and to teach others to do the same. A few claim she walks the beach continually searching for her little Angelino, but most insist she is contacting kindred spirits, people such as you, to ensure that her work and beliefs will continue.

Yes, as sure as we're sitting here now, the oddly dressed figure you experienced in the mist of the early morning was Margaret Fuller, in theory dead and gone these past hundred and fifty-six years. Now, tell me what she said.

Fire Island's First and Most Infamous Pirate

One of the more colorful characters ever to enliven the pages of our local history books is the notorious Fire Island land pirate Jeremiah Smith. He is recognized as the first permanent resident of Fire Island and, over time, has earned the more dubious distinction of being cited as the most infamous land pirate among a host of nefarious characters. Well-documented stories of his ruthless behavior have for nearly two centuries painted the picture of an evil man preying upon poor, shipwrecked souls and profiting from the spoils of ill-fated vessels helplessly grounded on the treacherous Fire Island sandbar.

I always thought of Jeremiah Smith in that way, until about a year ago when a friend showed me a copy of part of an old, non-attributed diary he had discovered, quite by accident, in the library of donated material at the New York Historical Society mansion on Central Park West in New York City. One word of caution: unsubstantiated comments from someone's diary are not the stuff on which historians rely. But for ordinary folks like you and me -- we can at least enjoy hearing what might well be the truth. If nothing else, this newly discovered testimony adds to our body of knowledge of the barrier beach and all its mysterious lore.

Most of the diary appears to have been written fairly late in Mr. Jeremiah Smith's decades-long career as a pirate, apparently by someone who worked either as a ship's mate or in some other intimate supporting role to Jem Raynor, a confederate of Mr. Smith's who transported Smith's ill-gotten gains from his beach house on Fire Island into New York City.

In a spidery script the diarist describes Jem Raynor, a young man who owned a sloop called the Intrepid, which was the mode of transport used to smuggle Smith's pirate booty covered under a heavy layer of the Great South Bay's finest quahogs.

Historical texts say that in the late 1700's Smith built his beach house not far from, if not immediately within, the business district of present day Cherry Grove. As the years passed, using only salvaged items from the shipwrecks, Smith improved his home until by the early 1800s it included two large living room windows. In 1868, Archie and Elizabeth Perkinson rebuilt Smith's home creating the first "shore-dinner" restaurant at the place they named Cherry Grove. The diary sheds no additional light on any of that.

Without further caution or description, let me relate to you some of the more interesting parts of this journal. You will read for yourself what this unfortunate associate of Jem Raynor had to say about Fire Island's premier pirate, the infamous Jeremiah Smith.

*   *   *

No one knows for certain from whence Smith originally came. Jem Raynor told me Smith was from somewhere on Long Island. The British Army orphaned him at a very young age. He and his family were some of the little-talked-about civilian casualties of the lengthy British occupation. More Jem does not know, and says, rightly enough, that a man is entitled to his privacy. Jem says no one could expect such a man to offer the particulars of what brought him to such a desolate place as Fire Island, penniless and alone, ready as a mere lad to take on the wild and unforgiving people and creatures that today still inhabit the place.

I will never forget the first time I saw him. It was an early summer morning with the wind blowing gently off a fog-shrouded sea, the kind of an early morning when the sound of a tern dropping headlong into the ocean in pursuit of some unwary baitfish might be heard from more than a hundred yards distant.

The stubble on his chin caught the mist of the morning air the way blades of beach grass catch the dew. The shimmering dampness served to emphasize sharp, angular facial features that framed narrow hawk-like brown eyes. His face seemed to portray a permanent mental state of extreme physical aggressiveness. At no more than average height, he was nonetheless an imposing figure, not just because of that face and those eyes, but also because of his very broad, powerful shoulders that slimmed to a narrow waist and hips. His naturally lean and muscular physique -- barely hidden under a ragged shirt and trousers -- had that smooth, sinewy look of one of the big cats on the hunt.

On this day Jem and I had sailed across the bay at an early hour. Two days prior, a barque had gone aground in a storm providing yet another opportunity to advance our livelihood. Of course, we do not engage in the immediate collection of treasure, leaving that to Smith who has a remarkable competence in gaining sole possession of the most valuable of cargos. We do not watch him at his trade; we are merely shippers providing a transportation service for goods that would otherwise go to waste. In order to secure spilled cargo he might occasionally be forced to employ techniques that border on being less than lawful, but that was none of our business.

We had arrived at Smith's house expecting to find him at home. He was not there, and so we reasoned he must be at the ocean beach. We thus proceeded in that direction to the top of a nearby dune.

Mr. Jeremiah Smith was on the beach in front of us, but he was not alone. He stood surrounded by four very sturdy and angry looking men. Who these men were, and what they wanted was anyone's guess, but when dealing with Jeremiah Smith most men wanted no witnesses of any kind. So for our own safety we quickly ducked behind the peak of the dune and watched to see the outcome of whatever this meeting was about.

What followed was nothing short of amazing. I have never seen any human being strike so fast in my life. When the man I will call number one raised his arm as if to attack, Smith flew at him catching him squarely on the jaw with his clenched right fist, causing the man's teeth to jump from his mouth like popcorn from fresh kernels thrown into a fire. The second man leapt to the defense of the first, but not in a style and manner sufficient to avoid Smith's counter blow: a well-placed kick that caught the man squarely in the groin lifting him full off the ground. But the third man, and possibly the strongest of the four, had gained enough time to be able to pull a knife and place it close to Smith's neck.

What happened next was almost certainly the sort of thing that has made the name Jeremiah Smith synonymous with evil. Somehow, Smith grabbed the man's wrist before he could strike, and with a steel-hard grip forced the dagger free from the man's hand. Then, with the speed and grace of a cat after a bird, Smith grabbed the fallen weapon and plunged it deep into the chest of its owner causing, most assuredly, near instantaneous death. He then turned to his other attacker and dispatched him as quickly and as cruelly as he had the first, slipping the blade of his own hunting knife into the soft flesh just under the jaw line. Such was the resulting blood and gore that the sand on which Smith stood looked like the sawdust on the floor of a slaughterhouse.

Jem and I were transfixed with the horror of what we had just witnessed and could do nothing for what seemed like several minutes; in reality it was probably no more than a few seconds. In all haste we retreated back from whence we had come, and without the necessity of uttering a word, agreeing between the two of us not to ever say a word to Smith or anyone else about what we had seen.

*   *   *

We don't know what happens after that because the man's diary slips to a considerably later date. In any case, our journalist and Jem Raynor appear to have continued their association with Smith despite the witnessed violence.

History books tell us Smith got married and had two sons with an obviously very brave and independent woman. But we never knew who this remarkable woman was, nor from where she came. How could a man such as Smith ever find, let alone marry, any woman? The mystery became only the greater because she is said to have died from drowning only three years after the marriage. Her death ended Smith's fearsome reign on Fire Island, because with the loss of his wife he was forced to care for his two very young boys all on his own. The history books say that one day he simply closed the door behind him, crossed the bay to Islip and, together with his two young boys, disappeared forever. The diary tells us a little more about Smith and his anonymous wife.

*   *   *

Two weeks ago, on the 5ᵗʰ of November to be precise, the paddle wheel steamer Savannah went aground in a great gale off Fire Place, just south of Old Inlet on Fire Island. She was a glorious ship, beautifully constructed and said to have all the most modern of amenities in her 32 staterooms. The Captain, an experienced fellow by the name of Mr. Holdridge, ran her flat aground close to shore where she took several days to break up in the pounding surf.

The local papers reported that eleven lives were lost. But it was not so. Jem and I learned just today that friend Jeremiah Smith had rescued more than his usual bundle of goods. He has with him now a quite striking young Norwegian girl who got separated from the others trying to reach shore from the doomed steamer and ended up exhausted and half drowned several miles down the beach. Smith found her, carried her back to his house and, rightly said, saved her from death by exposure. The two seem quite happy now and I would not be surprised to see something more permanent come of it.

*   *   *

That is all there is to the diary. Of course we know the date of the Savannah's loss as November 5, 1821. We also know that 11 passengers were reported drowned in the wreck. If we look up the identities of those lost we might be able to place a name to Mr. Smith's bride. What we do not know, and perhaps never will, is what happened to the infamous Mr. Smith and his two sons. Did he eventually become the mayor of a Long Island town as some assert, or did he just fade away?

The Lone Sentry

Not everyone who visits the Manor of St. George in Smith Point sees him, but over the centuries those who have say that Tom is a very handsome young man. Eye witnesses recognize him immediately, dressed in his 1780's British Army uniform, his long blond hair tucked under his black cocked hat, red coat with white facing, long white trousers, and a flintlock musket slung over his broad shoulders. They say Tom neither speaks nor gestures, but walks fitfully about, seeming to search for someone. And when the moon is full, some of those who see Tom say they hear the name "Rebecca" echoed in the rustling leaves of the trees that bend against the prevailing winds along the edge of the Great South Bay.

Tom, whose real name is known but to God, died at just after 4 a.m. on the morning of November 23, 1780. He was at his post, the lone sentry outside the British Fort at St. George's Manor at the far eastern end of the Great South Bay. Tom's duty was to guard, with his life if necessary, the fifty or so of his British army colleagues, and a number of Loyalists and their families sleeping in the safety of the fort's enclosure. Tom's orders were to sound the alarm if he saw anything suspicious, especially anyone who might be from General George Washington's rebel forces.

One particular guest at Fort St. George, Rebecca Hawkins, the eldest daughter in the family of deceased Loyalist Silas Hawkins, was reason enough for Tom to stay alert. Tom had known Rebecca and her family since shortly after hostilities had broken out. Rebecca's startling blue eyes, flaxen blond hair, and perfect form had attracted him at first, but it was her wit and intelligence that had taken Tom beyond his physical desire for her. While he knew fraternizing with local women was a punishable offense, Tom also knew the army needed every able man it had and that the officers could turn a blind eye to some regulations, particularly during time of war.

Every chance he got, Tom stole a visit with his beautiful Rebecca, their talk often turning to what seemed an impossible goal -- a happy and prosperous life together. They enjoyed playing what they called their game of "just supposing." Each would guess about what the other wanted for their own small farm, and how to manage the luxury of being dependent on nothing but their own hard work. Each found that their voiced dreams of a future together sustained them in the difficult present, and bound them far more closely together than might otherwise have been the case. They vowed their love for one another, and promised never to part.

In 1780, Loyalist troops had constructed Fort St. George. British army leaders had envisioned the fort not long after their 1776 victory over the Continental Army in the Battle of Long Island. The British needed the food supplies, timber, and hay

33

for their horses found on the eastern end of Long Island as well as a site from which troops could be quickly deployed. Fort St. George, built on a site overlooking the Great South Bay, included access to the deep-water channel from the mouth of the Carman's River out into the open ocean through Smith's Inlet (a place known today as Old Inlet).

Fort St. George was a triangular enclosure, several acres in size. Barricaded manor houses occupied two corners of the triangle with the actual fort in the third. The fort, a 90-foot square, had a deep ditch and high wall encircled by sharpened pickets. A stockade of pointed logs 12 feet high connected the fort with the two manor houses making the enclosure virtually impenetrable -- or so the British thought. Little did they know General George Washington's close friend and chief of his spy network, the 26-year-old Major Benjamin Tallmadge, had a plan to destroy it.

At 4 p.m. on November 21, 1780, Tallmadge, together with 80 dismounted dragoons, departed Fairfield, Connecticut in eight whaleboats. They rowed across the British-held Sound arriving at Old Man's (near today's Mt. Sinai Harbor) by 10 p.m. After hiding their whaleboats in the woods, they immediately began a cross-island march. But by 11 p.m. a heavy rain had set in, forcing Tallmadge to return his troops to the whaleboats. The contingent remained at Old Man's all night and through the next day until 7 p.m. The men then marched south arriving at 3 a.m. on November 23, about two miles from the British encampment.

While his men rested, Tallmadge met with Mr. William Booth, superintendent of the Manor of St. George. Booth had managed to convince the British he was a Loyalist while all the time actually working for Tallmadge's spy network. Booth briefed his leader on the layout of the fort, the details of the 50-man garrison, and the precise location of the one, lone sentry.

Just before 4 a.m., Tallmadge's men, in three groups, moved quietly through the forest toward the fort. Tallmadge thought the element of surprise to be so important that he ordered his men not to load their weapons but to rely only on their bayonets.

In the near total darkness, sentry Tom made out the shapes of the approaching armed men. He shouted out, "Who comes there?" He waited a moment. Was he mistaken? He heard the crack of a branch, and turned swiftly. "Who's there?" he yelled. Receiving no reply, he fired his single shot at the closest figure, missing his mark, but alerting those inside the fort.

No sooner had the smoke cleared Tom's gun than Sergeant Elijah Churchill, marching next to Tallmadge, seemed to appear from out of nowhere. With breathtaking speed Churchill drove his long, cold, steel bayonet through Tom's chest. For an instant Tom regarded his assailant with shock. How could this be? Tom dropped to his knees, his crimson blood streaming to the ground, his mind racing. As he felt his life force ebbing away, he could only think of finding Rebecca, to say one last good-bye. His last words were a vow, "I will find you, Rebecca. I must be with you."

With Tom's rifle shot, Tallmadge and the others had abandoned any pretense of stealth. They charged the fort yelling, "Washington and glory!" They quickly captured the main fort with no additional loss of life on either side. But then, with the patriot troops in celebration, shots rang out from the windows of both of the manor houses. Tallmadge ordered his troops to return fire, attack the houses and destroy the British opposition.

The fight became intense with vicious, hand-to-hand combat in both houses. Mercifully, only ten minutes after it had started, Tallmadge's troops gained control and the young commander ordered the fighting ended. A number of British soldiers and Loyalists -- including women -- lay seriously wounded. A half dozen of the British troops were dead, having been shot, or run through, and then, while immobilized, thrown out second story windows. Amazingly, the Americans suffered only one minor injury.

A witness to the entire proceeding from the nearby woods, William Booth, later described in his diary what he had seen. For reasons best understood by him, Booth most vividly remembered staring at the dying sentry. He said Tom took a long time to die, crawling toward the fort with his last ounce of life, calling out over and over again the name, Rebecca. That name was the last thing Booth remembered hearing him say before the wind drowned out his voice and life's spark abandoned his crumpled body. The handsome nineteen-year-old Tom died alone, an unlikely and unknown British army hero.

Rebecca Hawkins, who had been rounded up by the American force along with most of the other resident Loyalists, never learned what had happened to her young lover. Tallmadge's patriots immediately forced her and her family and most of the other Loyalists from the area warning them never to return again. No one knows where she went; no record exists of what ever became of her.

But each night, the lone sentry walks the grounds of St. George's Manor searching for his love, and the trees bend and sigh to the name Rebecca.

The Woman in the Black Velvet Dress

by Elaine Kiesling Whitehouse

 Young Zeke swung the sickle through the dry salt grass, gathering up bunches of it with his right hand and chopping it with his left. The curved metal of the blade glinted in the sun as Zeke raised it up and brought it down, over and over again through the marsh, cutting hay, a grim reaper in work clothes. He wore patched trousers, colorless with age, and a faded red shirt. His frowning sunburned face with its deep set, blue eyes made him look older than his 26 years.

Suddenly he stopped swinging his blade and squinted. He saw something lying in the grass, just ahead. Was it a deer, like the one he found last summer? No. This figure was all black, and its twisted posture was different. Zeke approached the figure. It was a woman. She wore a long, sodden, black velvet dress that was twisted around her body. Her head was turned so that her long, wavy black hair covered her face. Zeke nudged her with his toe. She was dead, just like the deer.

He rolled her head so that the hair fell away from her face. She was fair skinned and beautiful, but discoloration had started to set in. Mercifully, her eyes were closed. Strands of eelgrass clung to her hair and body. Her feet were bare.

Zeke just stood there staring, not knowing what to do. He put down his sickle and looked more closely. She seemed to be about his age. He bent down and lifted her left hand. She wore a ring set in gold, with a large red stone. Swirls of gold adorned each side of the ring. On impulse, he yanked it from her finger and put it in his pocket. Then he picked up his blade and went to tell the others what he had found.

Zeke always worked alone, apart from his brothers, who were right handed and used long handled scythes in tandem. They were working farther east along the marsh, near the edge of the bay. Mack and Ebon were still swinging their scythes, while Charlie and Hamish had already started to roll the hay into loose bales to drag to the barge.

Zeke ran up to them, not knowing how to begin to tell them what he had found.

"Where've you been?" asked Mack. His face was dark, annoyed. "We're fixing to leave before the storm blows up."

"Give me a hand here!" yelled Charlie.

Zeke did as he was told. He fingered the ring in his pocket, and then went to help the others pile hay on the flat barge. He would wait until the barge was loaded to tell them about the woman. He rolled hay into bales and dragged them to the barge, not saying a word. When at last the rickety craft was piled high and ready to be poled across the Great South Bay, he spoke up.

"I found a dead woman in the grass," he said.

The others didn't respond, so he stood there and said it louder: "I found a dead woman in the grass, wearing a black party dress."

Charlie stopped and took a pull from the cigarette that dangled from his mouth.

"Are you crazy?" He gestured toward the others. "Zeke here is so hard up for a woman that he says he saw one in a party dress in the hay. 'Cept she was dead. Haw Haw Haw!"

"It's true," Zeke insisted. "Come on, I'll show you."

The wind had picked up and white caps had started to form on the water.

"We'd best be getting back," said Hamish.

"I'll not leave 'til I show you this dead woman," said Zeke, crossing his arms over his chest."

"Aw, all right, said Charlie. "We'll be right back."

The two brothers set off to the spot where Zeke had found the body. He could see where he had cut the hay, but he did not see her.

"She was right here," he said, pointing to a spot in the marsh."

"Are you sure?" asked Charlie, who had long been aware of his brother's mental deficiencies. "You sure you didn't see a deer?"

"Naw. It was a woman. She was here." Zeke paused while Charlie took another pull on his cigarette. "Well, maybe there," he said, pointing a little further west. The two walked to that spot, but no body was to be found. Now Zeke became confused. Maybe Charlie was right. He usually was. Maybe there had been no woman in a black dress. But then he remembered the ring, and fingered it in his pocket.

"C'mon you stupid bastard," said Charlie. "We're leaving, before it blows up worse'n it is already." And Charlie stomped on ahead of Zeke. What could Zeke do, but follow?

The men got on the rickety barge and poled it across the Great South Bay. The prevailing southwest wind eased their way. The woman in the black velvet dress was forgotten. As for the ring, Zeke kept it a secret. He thought that if he showed it to the others, they would talk him into giving it to them. He would never see it again, and then he, too, would forget about the woman and how pretty she was, even if she was dead.

*   *   *

The room was silent for a moment, as I took in everything I had heard. The old woman telling the story had been looking out the window the entire time. Now she turned to face me, holding out her hand. On her third finger was a ruby ring set in gold, with swirls on either side.

"How did you end up with the ring?" I asked.

"When Zeke was old and sick he finally showed the ring to his brother Charlie, convincing him at last that he had found the woman in the marsh. Charlie was my great, great grandfather. The ring has been passed down in our family ever since."

But who was the woman?

"That remains somewhat of a mystery. After Zeke died, the story spread. A Wyandanch Indian heard of it and told Charlie that his ancestors -- members of his tribe -- had found the woman also, and had taken all her jewels, except for the ring, which they somehow had overlooked. They hid from the men who were cutting hay, and dragged her body away when Zeke left, leaving no trace behind. The Indian said her jewelry had the look of pirate booty, and that she must've been the consort of one of them, probably the captain, since none of the others could've afforded her. When the captain grew tired of her, he threw her overboard. Somehow she managed to swim to shore and drag herself over the dunes to the salt hay for shelter. But alas, she died of exposure. A while later the Indians, then Zeke, discovered her."

I listened in amazement. This was a fascinating tale, made real by this person who was related to the man who found the woman in the salt grass of Fire Island so many years ago.

"Thank you for telling me the story," I said. Now I will go home and write it so it is not forgotten, as was the poor woman in the black velvet dress."

*   *   *

In her book, *Fire Island 1650s-1980s* Madeleine C. Johnson mentions the mysterious woman in the black velvet dress.

The Face in the Rigging

On Friday morning, February 8, 1895, in a fierce gale and with temperatures holding near zero, the ice-encased 163-foot long three-masted schooner Louis V. Place went aground just off Cherry Grove. Soon after shuddering to a stop on the beach's outer bar, about a quarter of a mile off shore, the ship's ice covered deck came awash in the heavy seas. All eight crewmembers, including 58-year old ship's Captain William H. Squires, scrambled into the rigging, choosing the torture of exposure to the frigid winds to a quicker and more certain death in the waves crashing over the deck. The only question was whether or not any of the eight stranded men would live to tell the tale of how the five-year old vessel and her experienced crew arrived in such a dreadful predicament.

The potential for the loss of the entire crew did not come about for lack of rescue personnel. Despite extremely poor visibility, five minutes before the Place went aground, U.S. Life Saving Serviceman Fred Saunders, from his post on the beach, saw the ship headed for trouble. Saunders contacted the adjacent life saving stations for assistance and sent a messenger to his own crew who were already busy rescuing the crew of another three-master, the John B. Manning. The Manning had earlier gone aground about a mile east of where the Louis V. Place had hit bottom.

So it was not until about noon on the 8th that the rescue crews manned a Lyle gun in an attempt to set up for a breeches buoy rescue of the crew of the Place -- the ice, surf, wind and rip currents, making rescue by boat quite impossible. The lifesavers managed to get several lines over the ship, but because of the numbing effects of hypothermia, the stranded men did not have the dexterity to secure the lines.

The tall masts of the Manning and the Place could easily be seen from vantage points on Long Island's South Shore, and so word of the wrecks spread quickly. The Great South Bay was frozen over making it possible for the curious, the adventurous, and many who wished to try to help in some way, to trek to the scene. By the afternoon of the 8th, despite the frigid conditions, a crowd estimated to number as many as 1,000 had formed on the beach. But no one could do anything to help the eight poor souls who stood freezing in plain view only a quarter mile away. No one could do anything except watch as the men suffered their slow and agonizing deaths.

At the time of the grounding, air temperatures hovered between zero and plus four degrees Fahrenheit with a continuous wind speed over 50 miles per hour as measured at nearby facilities in Sandy Hook, New York City, and Block Island. These figures placed the wind chill in the stranded ship's rigging at somewhere around minus 30 degrees. Frostbite can occur under those conditions in less than 30 minutes. Heavy snow squalls came and went. Freezing spray from the 20-foot breakers continuously filled the air. The sea itself, reflecting days of extremely cold temperatures, carried "porridge ice" two feet thick at the surface.

Captain Squires was the first to die. As Captain he had been the last into the rigging having made sure everyone else was aloft. Several times the sea had seemed to wash over his position, completely drenching him. Observers noted that being wet in such frigid conditions Squires could not be expected to survive for very long. Within hours, and without his uttering a word, Squires dropped like a stone from his station in the rigging. The crowd let out a collective gasp as the relentless seas swallowed him up, the currents carrying his lifeless body further out to sea.

Respected by all who knew him for his personal integrity and skills as a seaman, Captain William Squires received even greater accolades from those who had labored as members of his crew. It was said that he would never ask a sailor to do something he would not do himself, and that he never failed to place the wellbeing of his crew above his own. So, while the conditions of February 8th could not have been more against his survival, those who knew him suggested Captain Squires might have fallen as quickly as he did because of the man he was. They said he may have died as much from the extreme shock of losing his ship, and surely his crew, as from the intense cold. The remains of Captain William Squires were not recovered until several days later, washed up on the beach some 30 miles to the east, ironically not far from his Bridgehampton home. He left behind his loving wife Carrie and two beloved young children, a son and daughter.

From the instant of her grounding, the huge breakers that crashed against the hull of the dying ship had churned up clouds of icy mist that hovered around the masts and rigging. At times the windswept frozen fog shrouded the ship giving the entire scene an aura of eeriness, almost as though the scene was not of this world. And so it was that not long after Captain William Squires disappeared into the sea that a number of reliable witnesses on shore pointed out what they thought was the image of a desperate man's face framed in the swirling mist between the fore and mizzen masts. Not everyone could see it, but many did and later swore to it. Those who knew him said the face was unmistakably that of the man from Bridgehampton, for certain the ship's captain, Mr. William Squires.

No one can really say if it was a case of life imitating art or art imitating life, but the most remarkable thing about the image was not that people saw it, but that a photographer managed to capture it on film. Forty-eight hours after Mr. Squires left his ship for the last time, photographer Martin Anderson produced a single black and white photograph that captured the drama of the weather and the wreck as it had been on the afternoon of February 8th. Clearly visible in the photo is the outline of a man's face framed by the mist swirling in the ship's rigging. To this day no one knows for certain whether Anderson purposely created the image to capture the story, or whether the photograph itself is responsible for the legend.

After the loss of Captain Squires, it surprised no one to see more men begin to die. The ship's cook, Charlie Morrison, was the next to go. Charlie came from Oakland Street in Brooklyn and was a native New Yorker. A gregarious man, he liked to cook and loved to eat what he cooked. As with his Captain before him, poor Charlie uttered not a sound as he fell headfirst from the rigging into the relentlessly pounding sea. Charlie Morrison would never be seen again, his body lost forever.

Just before dark, the crowd watched as a third crewman succumbed to the elements. The young ship's engineer from Rhode Island, Charlie Allen, appeared to literally give up the ghost, falling backward from his station on the mast, arms and legs outstretched as if in flight. His body was recovered about three weeks later just west of Moriches.

The tragedy of Charlie Allen's death was not lost on his friend and mentor, the 50-year-old Norwegian mate Lars Givby. Soon after Charlie Allen died, Lars Givby too fell from the rigging.

Givby, a strong man weighing in excess of 200 pounds, remained afloat for a brief time before disappearing under the crest of a large wave. His remains would eventually be found off Forge River.

No one else fell that Friday night but by early Saturday morning it was plain to see that the 28-year old seaman August Olson was nearing the end. Olson had tried for hours to climb into the crude shelter made by Soren Nelson and Claus Stuvens. The two had cut some of the lines holding the furled mizzen topsail and crept into the opening thereby protecting themselves them from the death dealing wind. Olson was just below the crosstrees holding Nelson and Stuvens, but the paralysis of his hypothermia prevented him from climbing just that little bit further to relative safety. Stuvens and Nelson could touch him and repeatedly reached out to try to help him, but to no avail. Olson died about 2 a.m., frozen to the mast and the rigging just below Stuvens and Nelson.

At daybreak it was plain to see that the young and handsome blond Norwegian, Fritz Ward, also had died sometime in the night. The only thing keeping him aloft was the ice and the lashings he had used to tie himself to the rigging; he was frozen solid to the ratlines, his handsome head rocking back and forth in the wind.

It was not until close to midnight on Saturday, more than 40 hours after the ship had gone aground that the storm and violent seas abated enough to allow the life saving service to launch a boat. With a Herculean effort the lifeboat crew of seven men managed to get alongside the wreck and bring Nelson and Stuvens down from their refuge and safely back to shore. The two were given food and water with Dr. George Robinson of Sayville making every effort to warm their bodies and save their lives. They were then transported for treatment to a hospital on Staten Island where Nelson, who had suffered severe frostbite, passed away only a few days later. After several weeks of recuperation, Stuvens recovered his physical health and returned to the sea, the only life he ever knew. However, he was said by many never to have been the same man again.

As for the life saving crew that performed so heroically that weekend, Keeper Sim Baker suffered severe frostbite of both his hands and feet and eventually contracted pneumonia from which he never recovered. He was not the only one to suffer; all those involved in the rescue from the life saving service suffered to some extent from frostbite and exposure.

Those were the kind of men who, in days gone by, dared to go down to the sea in ships and such were the men who stood vigil on the shore to save them when they could. They are all a part of Fire Island's great heritage.

Tala the Wolf

As early as the ninth century in the Middle East, Bedouins described the haunting sounds of the desert. They described the sounds as booming, roaring, or even musical. Of course, the sounds were produced by the prevailing winds and shifting sands of the desert dunes.

On Fire Island, however, Native Americans had another explanation for this mysterious acoustical energy. The sounds were not caused by the wind and sands, they said. The sound was the howl of Tala, a creature so fearsome that its reputation became legendary.

For centuries before the arrival of the Europeans, members of the black meadowlands, or Secatogue tribe and the "land beyond the hill" tribe—the Patchogue—came to Fire Island to catch the plentiful fish and shellfish, and to hunt the abundant right whale, deer, and seals. There were so many seals that the Indians called the barrier beach Seal Island.

The hunters always built a good fire, a fact sometimes cited as the reason for the name later given to the barrier beach. The fires signaled their location to family on the mainland, cooked and preserved their catch, rendered fat and whale blubber, and provided warmth from the chilly winds that buffeted the beach even in the warmer months. But the Indians also built fires for another reason—to protect themselves from the ravenous gray wolves that prowled this same rich hunting ground.

History tells us that the Native Americans respected the gray wolf, once found in most of North America, as a fellow hunter. They recognized the animal's intelligence and even his nobility.

But the gray wolf could be dangerous, not just because of his size and speed -- a big male stood almost three feet at the shoulder and could weigh as much as 150 pounds. The animal was cunning. The gray wolf could use all his advanced senses of smell, hearing and almost supernatural communication to defeat human competitors and capture his prey. When a big gray wolf howled victory over his conquered foe the eerie sound of his deep-throated call could be heard clearly across the Great South Bay and well into shore.

One Indian named Chogan related a story taken from events that happened centuries ago, a story about a wolf that lived alone in the forest swale between the high dunes and the bay on the great ocean beach. This was Tala. The name means wolf, but Chogan used other words for the creature. Chogan's words translate into something close to "man-animal." The story said that the Indians considered Tala uniquely evil among his kind. For many years the creature prevented all but the bravest and most fortunate of men from successful hunts. These hunters claimed Tala was more than a mortal beast. They believed he was the devil in earthly flesh.

Experienced hunters who had seen Tala reported him to be at least four feet at the shoulder with a weight greater than that of the largest of men. Instead of the gray, or gray-brown coloration of most of his species, he had a pure black coat of thick coarse fur, said to be as impenetrable to the sharpest of arrows as a turtle's shell is to a drop of rain. Those who had seen him up close and yet managed to survive said his most fearsome feature was his eyes -- immense, oval shaped yellow orbs that narrowed slightly toward a giant muzzle. The eyes were said to be clear, sharp and challenging, like those one might expect from an intelligent but evil being.

All wolves are built for stamina, but Tala was remarkable even among his kind. His deep chest and long, powerful back legs enabled him to run for miles and reach chase speeds faster than the swiftest deer. Also like all wolves, Tala had unusually large paws for the size of his body, making him able to better distribute his considerable weight over the sandy surfaces of the beach -- even on two legs.

It was Tala's ability to walk great distances upright, on his long hind legs like a man, that unnerved even the bravest of hunters. When standing on his back paws he was taller than any man. Shrouded in his black fur with his giant, ugly face framed in a great black ruff he looked like the devil himself. Seen at a distance in the mist of early morning, or in the twilight of evening (the only times anyone ever actually saw him) he was a terrifying presence.

The mere sight of him prompted many hunters to drop their catch and run for their lives. More than a few brave men lost their race with the hideous beast and died horrible deaths, with deep claw marks on every body part not torn off at the joints. The screams from those caught in his grasp lived forever in the minds of those that heard them. Hunters who found the victims' remains the next day said the pale dunes were streaked with crimson.

Chogan's story does not reveal what happened to the fearsome man-like beast, although it concludes with the ominous warning that perhaps it never died; it is still out there, animal or human, or some combination thereof. Over the centuries, unexplained deaths on the barrier beach, attributed to other causes, could have been the work of the evil, yellow-eyed monster.

While Chogan offered no additional detail or reference to define his story as much more than legend, recent discoveries may provide further insight into this gruesome tale. Within the past couple of years, historians have discovered diaries and other first-hand witness accounts from early European visitors and settlers to the northeast coast. These texts provide evidence that Native Americans probably traded with Basque and Celtic fishermen for centuries before the arrival of the historically documented European explorers of the early 16th century. The evidence further points to some limited Native American familiarity with European words and European cultural and historical phenomena.

European history from the same approximate timeframe as the story of Tala is replete with stories of lycanthropy. In almost every European country tales exist about the hideous doings of half-man and half-wolf creatures that today we know as werewolves. Is it possible that this Native American story about the beast that lived on Fire Island had some of its origins in those European cultures? We may never know.

But even today in France there is a common idiom—*entre chiens et loups*—to describe twilight. This is a time when it is impossible to tell a dog from a wolf, a friend from a foe, or perhaps a man from a beast.

Billy Boston

Some people know that Jupiter Hammon, a Lloyd family slave his entire life, was America's first published black poet, but almost no one knows about the man thought to be his son, a freed slave by the name of Billy Boston. The idea that Boston might be Hammon's son derives from several facts. First, Boston claimed his mother told him he was Hammon's son. Second, Boston could read and write despite having no known formal education. Third, he was about the right age to be Hammon's son. And finally, his last name was the same as the city that was home to Phillis Wheatley, the first published black woman poet, whom Hammon referred to as an Ethiopian poetess and whom he honored in 1778 with his second and best-known piece of published poetry. But whether or not Boston was Hammond's son is not as interesting as the story of Billy Boston himself.

Billy Boston was not only well read and well spoken, but he was also a giant of a man. In height he stood a good measure more than six feet and weighed the equal of two full-grown men. His massive shoulders measured about the width and breadth of an oak-stave barrel turned on its side and each of his thighs were almost twice the thickness of ordinary men at the waist. As for his intellect, he knew enough about the world and the Christian religion to qualify as a student of Hammon's mentor, the Harvard-educated Nehemiah Bull.

Boston told folks he had been freed in 1788, shortly after the New York State legislature passed a law permitting owners to free their slaves. At first, his inclination had been to leave the area entirely, but since he did not have much money, and without any particular place to go, he decided to remain close to the Great South Bay and the coastal home he had known during the first forty years of his life.

Like Hammon, Billy Boston was a deeply religious man and in his free time enjoyed preaching the gospel to black, South Shore congregations just as Jupiter Hammon had done on the Lloyd Manor Estate. Boston subscribed to Hammon's famous words from a speech given in 1786 when he said, "If we should ever get to Heaven, we shall find nobody to reproach us for being black, or for being slaves." Boston's sermons sounded like Hammon's, with the theme that blacks should maintain high moral standards because their slavery on earth had guaranteed them a place in Heaven.

These were dangerous times for a man such as Billy Boston. He was a free man, but many citizens in early 19th century America did not accept freedom for any black person. Worse yet, a criminal element kidnapped free blacks and sold them back into slavery in the South. These evil men were known as "blackbirders."

Billy Boston was more at risk from blackbirders than most freed slaves for a number of reasons. First, he could read, write and carry his own with any gentleman of the time. In the South he would be of value as a house slave. Second, his physical strength made him the equivalent of two or more normal sized field hands; and third, he was as gentle as he was big.

The blackbirders came for him in the night, long before the roosters had given any consideration to announcing the new day. It must be said that Boston did not give up without a fierce struggle; in fact, even in his somnambulant state he was able to inflict considerable physical damage to at least three of his kidnappers before finally succumbing to the brute force of some half-dozen strong men.

They tied him hand and foot, gagged him with a sock, placed a hood over his head and then threw him into a large wagon, covering him with a thick layer of hay. The trip to the landing on the Connetquot River took less than a half an hour. Before sunrise Boston was out of the wagon and loaded onto the sloop "Early Bird" for the voyage to what is today known as Ocean Beach.

By noon that morning the sloop was approaching Fire Island Inlet and the western reaches of the then isolated and desolate western end of the great barrier beach. Invisible to the approaching boat, or any prying eyes for that matter, was the guardhouse and stockade in which the blackbirders kept their human cargoes. Concealed between two dunes stood the fairly sizeable facility, which, at least on one map dated January 1, 1798, is simply identified as the James Smith House.

As is well known, William Tangier Smith originally owned all of Fire Island and the Great South Bay. Upon his death in 1705, his oldest son Henry inherited all the property from Long Cove in the east to Fire Island Inlet in the west. This land stayed in the family until 1779 when Henry Smith's great grandson inherited it and promptly sold it to "twenty yeomen of Brookhaven" for 200 pounds sterling. Lost in the fog of history are the identities of the "twenty yeomen," and so it is with the real identity of the owner of the slave stockade probably as described on the map from 1798 as the James Smith House.

In any case, the blackbirders unloaded Billy Boston from the sloop, everyone wading ashore to make their way up the lonely dunes to the hidden stockade. Once inside they removed Boston's ropes, replacing them with iron leg and wrist shackles that were securely attached to the brick walls. Here Billy Boston would sit, in his manacles and chains, until a coastal trader was ready for the trip south and the lucrative slave markets of the pre-Civil War.

Today we know about the Ocean Beach stockade thanks to Douglas Tuomey, a well-known Fire Island historian who in 1907 accompanied Mr. John Wilbur to Fire Island to look at a site where Wilbur planned to build a hotel. At the time, this site, which Wilbur intended to name Ocean Beach, was basically barren except for the Fire Island lighthouse and the rusting hulk of what was the Western Union tower.

Tuomey recalls that on that late summer day in 1907, laborers at the site of the proposed hotel were using a primitive device known as a scoop to excavate the foundation. Two mules, attached to what looked like a huge sugar or flour scoop, pulled loads of soft sand out of the increasingly deep hole. But suddenly, at a depth of about eight feet, the scoop caught on the edge of some large, immovable object causing the scoop to tip over and the mules to break harness and bolt for the brush. After the commotion had subsided, Mr. Wilbur ordered his workmen to use hand shovels to uncover what appeared to be the leading edge of some sort of larger brick structure.

Tuomey writes that they eventually uncovered a hearth ten or twelve feet long and four feet deep with heavy charred timbers and large bolts and spikes. Obviously, a substantial building had once stood precisely in that spot. About a foot from the fireplace the workmen uncovered an iron kettle, and near that a pile of light iron chain, badly rusted, and other pieces of rusted ironwork, which because of its round shape might have been manacles or leg irons.

After much examination of all the facts, in 1958 Tuomey finally concluded, after consultation with other local historians, that the building had served as the guardhouse of the stockade in which slave traders kept their human cargoes until they could be shipped out without interference from the authorities.

In 2006, archaeological and anecdotal evidence came to light indicating the existence of a man not unlike the legendary Billy Boston described above. This information describing the man's near super-human physical strength has caused news accounts to refer to him, whoever he might really be, as the Black Paul Bunyan.

Another Turn of the Screw

by Elaine Kiesling Whitehouse

I accepted the position as governess at the lighthouse as a lark. I saw the job as an adventure and a challenge. My duties would consist of caring for and teaching the two small children of the lighthouse keeper, whose wife had died suddenly not long ago. I tried to imagine what it was like for two youngsters to live in a lighthouse, at the west end of Fire Island, with only an occasional visitor and no school nearby. The Keeper's brother had made the arrangements with me in New York, telling me only that the two children, a boy and a girl, had lost their mother and that the former governess had quit after only a week. The keeper, a Mr. Daff, needed someone sturdy and willing to stay for at least the remainder of the school term – two months.

For two months I supposed I could do anything. I planned to work with the children, ages eight and five. I would draw and paint watercolor scenes of the beach, and keep notes in a journal to perhaps publish a record of my adventure one day. In fact, this is the story which you will read, but it is not at all what I expected.

Once I saw all the work a lighthouse keeper had to do I understood why I seldom saw him. He would climb the 180 steps at least three times a day. At sundown he would light the lamps, at midnight he would check the oil supply, and at sunrise he would extinguish the lamps. The giant lens had to be cleaned of soot, and its brass fittings checked and polished. The oil lamps had to be cleaned and filled, and the wicks trimmed. The windows had to be washed and the steps had to be swept. He had to keep a log of weather conditions, equipment problems, and anything unusual he spotted at sea. He had to report any shipwrecks and, although there were almost none, rescues.

Yet as time went on, despite all the work he had to do, I found it strange how little interest Daff took in his own two children. What had happened to their mother? I wondered. Albert, the eldest, simply told me that she died. The little one, Imogene, had already started to forget. And despite caring for the children – making their meals, changing their beds, teaching them their lessons – I felt there was a wall between us. They did as they were told, yes, but as soon as their lessons were done they left the little schoolroom as soon as possible to run up the steps to the room over the portico, where they played. Sometimes the laughter and noise was astounding – I felt the two were having a very good time, indeed. But when I came to check on them, rapping lightly, the laughter stopped and I opened the door to find them sedately thumbing through a book, or looking out the window. I did not understand this at all.

"What were you playing?" I asked. "It sounded like such fun."

Albert shrugged his shoulders. "Nothing, really."

What about you, Imogene?" A little frown creased her pretty forehead, as if considering what to say.

"We were playing with . . . and . . .

Albert interrupted, "Her imaginary friends," he said.

Of course! I realized that children as isolated as Imogene and Albert would invent playmates. Imaginary friends were extremely common. I thought perhaps it was time to take them to the mainland for an outing. I would ask their father that evening.

I saw him at the dinner table, where he usually ate quickly alone before returning to his room or his tasks. The children always had their dinner an hour earlier.

"Mr. Daff," I said. "I think it would do Albert and Imogene some good to get away for a day. Perhaps you could take us to the mainland on the next bright day, early in the morning, and meet us again after lunch. I think they would so enjoy a picnic . . ."

He stared at me with a look I could not decipher, but suffice it to say it was cold. "That is not the plan," he said. "You are to remain here with the children. I cannot risk allowing them to go to shore."

"But, they need to meet other children, to see other people . . . It would only be for a few hours," I said.

He waited for me to finish, then narrowed his eyes and said, "No. That was not in the plan when I hired you." Then he got up and left.

I didn't know what to think. Perhaps he was so fearful since his wife had died that he was afraid something awful would happen to his children as well. I could understand that. I decided to try again another time. Now it was time to get the children ready for bed.

I walked up the steps to the portico room, where their shrill laughter grew louder and louder. What on earth were they doing? Perhaps I should not leave them alone in there, unsupervised. Yet the room was perfectly safe – no sharp objects, only books and toys. The window was always shut against the wind at this time of year, and it was much too heavy for them to open.

This time I did not knock, but opened the door quickly. The children were sitting on the floor, with a board game between them. They looked up at me and blinked.

"What were you doing?" I asked.

"Playing," said Albert. But I noticed a lowering of his eyelids, and Imogene quickly looked over her shoulder, as if to see if someone were there. Albert was lying. But why?

"Why don't you tell me what is so funny?" I asked softly. "I could use a good laugh, too, you know."

The children shrugged, and at that moment I felt as if a cold hand were placed on my arm. The experience sent a shot of adrenaline through my body and momentarily took my breath away. What was going on? Ghosts? Nonsense! I stood up and said, "Albert, Imogene, I insist that you tell me what you've been doing and who you've been with!" but the children just looked up at me and blinked.

Suddenly I sensed another presence in the room. I swung around to see the lighthouse keeper standing in the doorway.

"Is something wrong?" he asked.

The two children ran to him and hugged his legs, looking at me with wide eyes. What could they possibly have to fear? I wondered.

"No, everything is fine," I said. But everything was not fine.

During the next weeks matters got gradually worse. Yes, I taught the children their lessons. I took them for walks along the beach. But all the while I sensed they were holding something back. I grew worried and began having headaches, some of them excruciating, forcing me to retreat to my room and remain there with the shutters closed. As I lay there, I could hear the shrieking and laughter in the room above, and I began to wonder if I was losing my mind.

A few nights later I woke up in the middle of the night. Albert and Imogene were standing in my doorway. I got out of bed. I felt certain that something was wrong, for they had never done this before. They stood there, in their little white nightgowns, shivering.

"What is it, children?" I asked, bending low to them and putting my arms around them. They turned around and pointed to the hall, saying nothing. Albert led the way out of the room, heading toward the tower steps. He tugged on my nightgown despite my protests. I had never climbed to the top, and to do so now in my long nightdress seemed absurd. But the children clung to me and I relented.

We went up single file, with Albert leading the way, and Imogene holding my hand behind me. Halfway up, I stopped. My heart was beating and I was slightly short of breath. Beads of perspiration formed on my forehead. Albert waited a moment, and then continued. Finally we reached the top.

The sight of the giant lens was something to behold. It turned on its axis, its beacon reaching out to the sea, cutting into the fog like a blade, and changing its color from gray to sulphurous yellow as it passed. I thought of the ships out there that might be in peril. I prayed that their captains would be guided by the light and be safe.

And then I saw her, standing at the opening, her ghostly pallor and white hair leaving no doubt that she was not part of this earth. She beckoned to me and the children. Had she been calling to them each night? They went to her while I stood frozen, not believing my eyes. She led them to the trap door that opened out to the ledge surrounding the tower, into the fog. She held out her hands to the children, and nodded her head for me to follow. I was seized by a sense of losing my will, and stepped out on the ledge, with Albert and Imogene clinging to my nightgown. I was in a nightmare where I could not move or run away. Just one little push and the children would go over the edge. Just one more step and I would follow. A blinding pain seared through my head, like the flash of the beacon, and with it the realization that the ghost wanted the children to join her. I summoned my strength and hugged them to me, pulling them back inside, and ran with them, sobbing, all the way back down the steps. This demented woman, their mother, had leapt to her doom from the tower, and now she wanted to take her children with her. The evil of it all was too horrifying for contemplation.

I kept Albert and Imogene with me in my bed that night, shivering until the morning sun streamed in the window. They were asleep when I marched into Mr. Daff's study and told him I was resigning and that the children were not safe in this place. He sighed, and said he understood, but that the children would stay, after all, they were his children.

That day I packed my bags, kissed the children, and left. I was sorry to leave them, but my own wellbeing precluded remaining there.

And so, I have written all this down. Sad to say, within the year, both children died in a tragic fall from the tower, along with their governess whom some say lost her mind from the isolation of living in the lighthouse, and pushed them over the edge.

A Greater Spirit

Rick phoned to say he was in town, needed a place to stay, and wondered if I might put him up for a few days at my place in the Pines. Sure, what the hell, he was an old friend, I hadn't seen him in ten years or more and besides, what harm could it do?

What harm would it do? The question took up residence somewhere in the back of my mind -- something someone had said years ago about Rick. Was it that he traveled too much? Something about his life style caused mutual friends to wonder if maybe Rick was into something better left unsaid. But the last I'd heard, he had a good job, and so I assumed the gossip mill was just operating as usual. I agreed to meet him at the Pines ferry dock.

As I sat waiting for the Sayville ferry to make its way into the harbor, I thought about my day at the ocean. An unusual nor'easter, a storm almost unheard of at this time of year, had moved out to sea. The wind and waves carted away layers of sand and had exposed a real hidden treasure, something a scientist would love to examine. A large section of the side and deck of an ancient ship appeared out of the surf, on the edge of the beach, at low tide. The ship, now just black remains, must have been resting undisturbed in its Fire Island grave for a very long time. Beautifully handcrafted, curved bronze nails and a few heavier bronze rods held the massive, hand-hewn oak timbers together. Despite a lifetime around boats and ships, I had never before seen work like it. This piece of history would not long remain where it lay, and like so many things at the beach, it was meant to be enjoyed in the moment. Soon the sea would take back what it had decided to share, if only for a short while.

As I saw the ferry approaching in the distance, my thoughts drifted to my memories of Rick's parents, who had passed away some years ago. They had been so proud of their Dutch heritage, claiming the family had come to America aboard a Dutch ship in the late 1600's. I even remembered the name of the ship -- the *Prins Maurits* -- because I had found their story so intriguing. They said the ship, loaded with people looking to settle in the New World, went aground in the early spring on Fire Island somewhere near the present locations of Fire Island Pines or Cherry Grove. Miraculously, in the bitter cold and dark, everyone aboard had survived the shipwreck. Some people attributed the survival of the Dutch passengers and crew to efforts by the local Secatogue Indians and what Rick's parents referred to as the "Greater Spirit." Could the wreck on the beach be this ship? I wondered.

The ferry pulled smoothly alongside the dock. As Rick disembarked I noticed that he had always been thin, but now he seemed even more so. His hair was longer, brought back in a ponytail. His clothes would have let him go unnoticed in any Mexican border town. And when he came close and shook my hand, I thought how with old friends, the years pass and the person looks completely different, but there is something about the eyes that doesn't change. But despite the physical appearance, his personality was the same, and I soon found myself glad to welcome him into my home. He let me know how much he appreciated the hospitality and said that after a few days of rest and quiet he would again be on his way.

At first, Rick seemed to enjoy just hanging out in the house, not wanting to go out except to visit the beach in the very early hours. But by the evening of the second day, he began to open up. That night, over drinks and dinner, we talked about mutual friends and our travels. I told him I had just retired from government service in a job that had required lots of international travel.

Rick said he too had traveled extensively, mostly in Mexico and Central America, but also in Europe, and as far east as Istanbul. We both knew some of the same little hotels on the Bosphorus, and the ones overlooking Topkapi and the Golden Horn. We had both stayed at the charming old Pera Palas. In the old days this was where you spent the night after getting off at the last stop on the Orient Express.

As we settled into one more after dinner drink, Rick paused, looked at me as if weighing his options, and then slowly began to tell his story. He reminded me that his parents had always told him his Dutch last name and tall good looks would help make him successful. And failing that, he said with a laugh, he could rely on what his parents had insisted on calling the "Greater Spirit," who shepherded his ancestors miraculously to America hundreds of years ago.

He said that for a long time he had been doing a second business on the side. It was this business that had brought him to the Pines. He said his job was to provide a unique service, and while he made a lot of money, it was the customer who received the most benefit. He said he made it possible for the best minds and the most creative people in the country to function at a higher level. He implied that he was part psychiatrist, part spiritual leader and part entrepreneur.

Despite his success, he said, many people were blind to the real benefits to America that his service provided. These people were basically from regressive elements within our society. They not only worked to hurt his business, but also to destroy him personally and others like him, who help people achieve the highest forms of art, music, dance and other great human achievements.

Sure, Rick admitted, some people developed a problem with what he sold, but people have always had problems with mind-altering substances. He admitted he had lost some friends who made mistakes, but that was a small price to pay for the overall benefits to society.

I cut him off. I just couldn't bear to hear any more about what Rick had become. Sitting in silence for what seemed like a long time, I began to realize that while part of me literally wanted to throw Rick out the door, another part was telling me there were things I needed to know. For one thing, it was obvious that Rick did not come to the beach for a rest. He came to hide either from those who would do him harm or from the law, or maybe even to do a deal. Hell, some of my good friends in law enforcement were probably out looking for him now.

Rick could read my thoughts. "Look," he said, "I came here because you and I have been friends forever. I need you to let me stay for just another day or two. I know you have dedicated your life to serving good old Uncle Sam, but I also know you're smart, and you value a true friendship. I'm betting my life you won't turn me in. Look, I don't have stuff with me and I'm not packing. Only you know I'm here. Please let me stay and then I'll be safe and on my way again."

Not really sure I was doing the right thing or even what I wanted to do, I reluctantly agreed to let him stay another two days, but only if he told me exactly what had brought him to the Pines.

He said he had come because of a recent problem with someone who had been a longtime customer. The man had somehow lost his mind, and in a rage ended up killing his wife and their three young children. A few powerful people outside the law had threatened to kill him. Not only that, the police were after him for what he knew about this guy and his family as well as some other incidents. Rick said he had come here because he knew he could trust me and, strange as it might sound, he felt drawn to this part of the beach by something he could not explain.

That night I could not sleep trying to decide what to do. I knew I had to go to the law, but as I saw Rick drifting off to sleep, he looked just the way I remembered him as a childhood friend -- an innocent boy dozing on the ferry as it eased back toward the mainland.

By morning I had made up my mind. I decided I would talk this over with Warren, my old Suffolk County cop friend, first thing. Rick would be off on his early morning visit to the ocean and I would be free to leave the house without explanation. I could speak to Warren confidentially and between the two of us we would figure out what to do. I hoped there would be a middle ground; something between turning in a friend to face what would amount to a death sentence, and stopping what would be a death sentence for others if Rick were allowed to go on. Warren would help me find the solution to this devil's riddle.

Warren was never too busy to talk, but this morning seemed like it might prove the exception. As I entered his outer office, I could tell something big had just happened. It sounded like Warren was summoning every resource available to him. The phones didn't stop ringing. He was talking to someone from the Pines Fire Department, the radio was crackling with the police boat, and some Fire Island National Seashore ranger was on another line.

Just then Warren saw me and motioned me into his office. As I sat there and listened, it became obvious that something had happened at the ocean. Warren spoke with me as though I was on one of his communications links, like I'd been there from the start of whatever had occurred.

"Regardless of how much I argue for lifeguards at the Pines, they won't listen," he said, shaking his head. "Maybe when something like this happens --- maybe now they will. Some guy -- no identification -- got caught in a really bad riptide and was sucked out to sea, just about ten minutes ago! A couple of people on the beach said they had never seen a rip that bad. Must have been leftover from that nor'easter the other night, the same one that brought up that old ship. In fact, happened right in the same location! The sea took this guy, just like that, without a trace."

About the Author

Jack Whitehouse has spent most of his life on or near the water. He first visited Fire Island as a child in the early 1950s and remains a regular visitor to this day. In 1955 he took his first sailing lesson on the Great South Bay eventually teaching sailing for the Wet Pants Sailing Association in the early 1960s.

Receiving his commission in the U.S. Navy in 1968, he then served aboard the destroyer U.S.S. Buck for two cruises to Vietnam. In 1971 he became the Executive Officer and then the Commanding Officer of the patrol gunboat U.S.S. Chehalis sailing out of Guantanamo Bay, Cuba.

In the early 1970s, following Norwegian language training, he became the first U.S. Navy exchange officer with the Royal Norwegian Navy serving for a combined total of 20 months in Norwegian frigates, patrol boats and submarines in waters north of the Arctic Circle.

Jack is currently working on a second book: a history of the home for children, known as the "Cottages," in Sayville, Long Island. He also writes for the Fire Island Tide under the pen names Jay D. Raines and Lee Jouvet.

CPSIA information can be obtained
at www.ICGtesting.com
Printed in the USA
FFOW04n2227010415
12332FF